Zeke Meeks is published by
Picture Window Books
A Capstone Imprint
1710 Roe Crest Drive
North Mankato, MN 56003
www.capstoneyoungreaders.com

Best.
Game.
EVER.

Library of Congress Cataloging-in-Publication Data
Green, D. L. (Debra L.), author.
   Zeke Meeks vs. his big phony cousin / by D.L. Green; illustrated by Josh Alves.
      pages cm. — (Zeke Meeks)
   Summary: As if coming up with a school project at the last minute is not enough trouble,
Zeke also has to deal with his cousin Sam — who is just too perfect to be completely
believable.
   ISBN 978-1-4795-2167-8 (hardcover) — ISBN 978-1-4795-3812-6 (paper over board) —
   ISBN 978-1-4795-3810-2 (paperback) — ISBN 978-1-4795-5235-1 (ebook)
1. Cousins—Juvenile fiction. 2. Middle-born children—Juvenile fiction. 3. Elementary schools—
Juvenile fiction. [1. Cousins—Fiction. 2. Middle-born children—Fiction. 3. Schools—Fiction. 4.
Humorous stories.] I. Alves, Josh, illustrator. II. Title. III. Title: Zeke Meeks versus his big
phony cousin. IV. Series: Green, D. L. (Debra L.) Zeke Meeks.
   PZ7.G81926Zc 2014
   [Fic]—dc23   2013028540

Vector Credits: Shutterstock
Book design: K. Carlson

Printed in China by Nordica
0514/CA21400801
052014   008217R

Grace Chang:
Super Genius
or Super Villain?

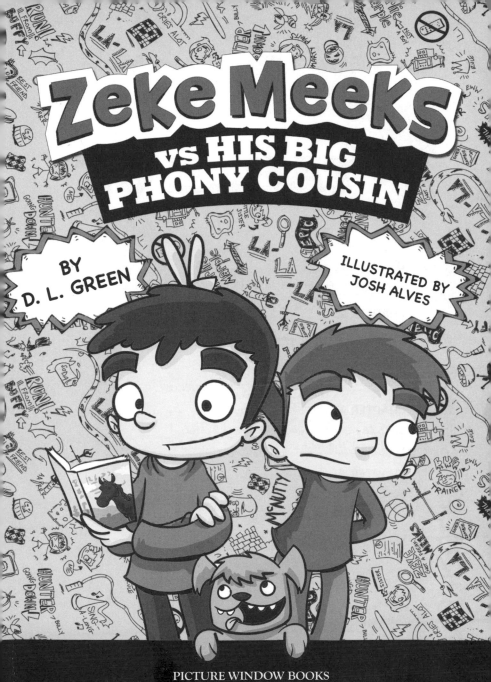

Zeke Meeks
vs HIS BIG PHONY COUSIN

BY D. L. GREEN

ILLUSTRATED BY JOSH ALVES

PICTURE WINDOW BOOKS
a capstone imprint

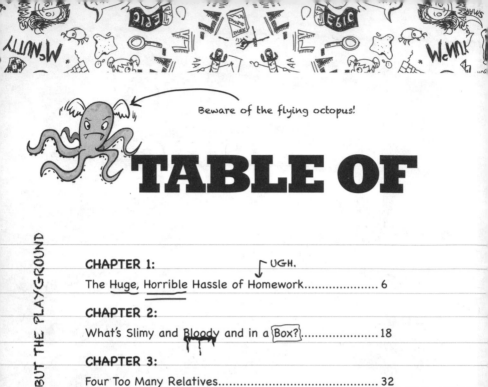

Beware of the flying octopus!

TABLE OF

Bad, bad idea.
Trust me.

BOYS RULE EVERYTHING BUT THE PLAYGROUND

This is Robot Rupert.
He may look cool,
but he is NOT cool.

CONTENTS

SERIOUSLY. You will be jealous.

GIRLS DROOL ALL BUT GRACE — SHE BITES

Which side are you on?

There should be a law against homework. After a hard day of goofing off in school, I shouldn't have to do more hard work. And I try very hard not to. But trying very hard to avoid work is hard work.

In class today, my teacher, Mr. McNutty said, "I hope you've all been working on your big homework projects."

I hadn't. I hadn't even started.

"This is the first time you've gotten to choose your own projects. They will show off your talents and interests. I look forward to seeing them and hearing your reports about them." Mr. McNutty pointed to the poster on the wall that said "Dare to Aim High." He stated, "Make sure you aim high and work hard."

There was that awful word again: *work*. Work just wasn't working for me.

"Each day, a few students will report on their big projects. Who wants to go first?" Mr. McNutty asked.

I raised my hand to offer to give my report last.

"All right, Zeke, you can go first," my teacher said. "Who wants to be second?"

I kept my hand up. I needed to explain that I wanted to be last.

But Mr. McNutty kept ignoring me and calling on my classmates.

Finally, everyone signed up to do a report.

I still had my hand raised.

"What is it now, Zeke?" Mr. McNutty asked.

"I want to give my report on the last day," I said.

"But you offered to go first a few minutes ago. You changed your mind already?" Mr. McNutty sighed. "All right, Zeke. I'll move you from the first day to the last day."

Now I had extra days to worry about the big homework project I hadn't started. I had no idea what project to do. I thought about doing a fake project. I could point to the air next to me and tell the class I'd built an invisible race car or rocket ship. I could even pretend to get in it and buckle an invisible seat belt.

No. Mr. McNutty wouldn't believe me. He'd probably give me a very visible punishment, like missing recess all week.

I spent a lot of time at school trying to think of ideas for the big project. I couldn't come up with anything.

When I got home, I took a break from thinking. I played my *Hit Everything that Moves* video game. Suddenly, I got a great idea for my project: I could show the class my video game skills. I'd worked hard at *Hit Everything that Moves*. I'd gotten to level 23 and earned a score of 463,916.

My little sister, Mia, started singing a song from *Princess Sing-Along*, her favorite TV show. Ugh. It was my least favorite show. There was only one thing worse than hearing Princess Sing-Along sing in her screechy voice: hearing my sister sing in her even screechier voice.

Mia sang, "Playing video games, la la la, can destroy people's brains, la la la."

"So can watching too much TV," I said.

"I'll keep watching my favorite TV shows: *Teens in Love* and *Bathing Suit Guys*," my older sister, Alexa, said. "I don't care if my brain gets destroyed."

"That's because you don't have a brain," I told her.

Mom turned off my game console and said, "Zeke, that's not nice. Go do your homework."

"I am doing my homework. I have to work on a big project. My big project is this video game. I'm going to show the class how well I play *Hit Everything that Moves*."

Mom shook her head. "Playing a video game is something you do for fun. It's not work. It doesn't count as homework."

I groaned.

Waggles, our dog, rested his head on my leg. He was trying to cheer me up. My sisters had tied pink ribbons all over his fur. That did not cheer me up.

"Cheer up, Zeke," my mom said.

I shook my head. Nothing could cheer me up today.

"Your cousin Sam is coming to visit tomorrow," she said.

I cheered up. Sam was my age. I hadn't seen him in years because he lived far away. But I knew we'd have fun together. We could play video games and basketball and have burping contests. My friends could meet him, too.

I couldn't wait to have another guy around. My dad was a soldier who was on a mission in another country. So I was the only guy in my house now besides my dog, and he was wearing pink ribbons.

"Your cousin Jen will be here, too," Mom said.

I cheered up even more. Jen was my sister Mia's age. I hoped Jen would keep Mia too busy to sing Princess Sing-Along songs.

"Sam and Jen don't have school this week," Mom said.

"I'll miss school this week to keep them company," I said.

Mom shook her head. "No, Zeke."

Oh, well. It was worth a try.

"What are you going to do for your big homework project?" Mom asked. Did she have to remind me?

"I could show off my art skills." I pointed to my painting on the refrigerator.

Mom scratched her head. "I was wondering about that picture. Is that a blue snake hiding in a brown shoe? Or is it blue spaghetti on a brown plate?"

It was supposed to be a picture of the seashore. I couldn't show off my art skills. I didn't have any art skills. I would never think of a homework project.

Mia sang in her screechy voice, "Homework will make you smart and cool, la la la. If you don't do it, you're a fool, la la la."

Well, then, I was a fool.

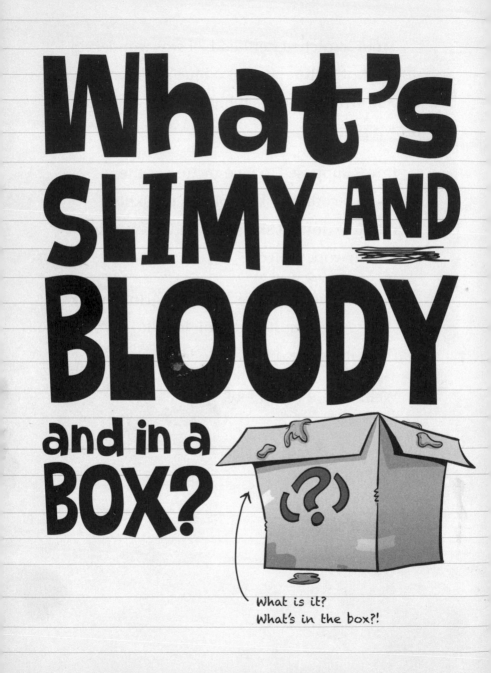

At school the next day, Victoria Crow gave her report first. She stood in front of the class and said, "I did a simple project. Of course, I am the smartest kid in third grade, so what's simple for me is very hard for other kids. I built a robot. He's better than a real person. He does exactly what I tell him to do. And he never has to eat or sleep or go to the bathroom or fart." She called out, "Yoo-hoo, Robot Rupert! Open the door and come in, please!"

Our classroom door opened. A big silver robot rolled into the classroom. He had claws instead of hands, and wheels instead of feet.

Victoria said, "I made Robot Rupert myself. He's made of six types of metal, lots of computer parts, an old toaster, and my sister's cell phone. Don't tell my sister. She's been looking everywhere for it." She pointed to the robot and said, "Rupert, please come here."

Rupert rolled over to her.

Victoria said, "Rupert, please tell the students about yourself."

Rupert said, "I was created by Victoria Crow. *Beep.* She is the smartest kid in third grade. She gave me life. *Beep.* Also, she gave me her sister's cell phone. Do not tell anyone. *Beep.*"

"Rupert, please clean the classroom." Victoria put a cloth in the robot's left claw.

Rupert stretched out his thin wire arms and rolled around the classroom. He picked up a pencil from the floor and handed it to Laurie Schneider. He used the cloth in his claw to polish Aaron Glass's shoes. He fluffed up Mr. McNutty's hairpiece.

"Does anyone have questions?" Victoria asked.

"Does the robot get along with pets?" I asked.

Victoria said, "My robot —"

Rupert cut her off. "I get along well with dogs, except the ones that drool. Drool can damage my system. Also, it is just plain disgusting. *Beep.* I do not care for cats. They jump on me and scratch me. Victoria has a cat named Nancy. I call her Nasty. That is because she is nasty. *Beep.* Sometimes I call the cat Idiot. That is because she is an idiot. *Beep.*"

"Thank you, Rupert," Victoria said.

"I do not like horses either," the robot said.

"That's enough, Rupert," Victoria said.

Rupert ignored her. "Horse poop is huge and stinky. *Beep.*"

I whispered to my friend Hector, "That robot is annoying."

Rupert pointed to me. "I heard that. If I had feelings, I would feel bad. Luckily, I do not have feelings. *Beep.* If I did, I would despise pigs and gerbils. They are ugly."

"Turn that thing off," Mr. McNutty said.

Rupert kept talking. "Now I will discuss fowl. *Beep.* That includes ducks, chickens, parakeets, cockatoos, mynah birds, turk—"

Victoria pressed a button on Rupert's belly. He finally stopped talking.

Everyone clapped.

I couldn't wait to tell my cousin Sam about the annoying robot.

Grace Chang walked to the front of the room and said, "Move out of my way. It's my turn to give my report."

"Yeah. It's Grace's turn," Emma G. said.

"Yeah. It's Grace's turn," Emma J. said.

Victoria returned to her seat.

Grace pointed to a huge box in the back of the classroom.

"Do you want me to have Robot Rupert bring that to you?" Victoria asked.

Grace shook her head. "Emma G. and Emma J. will do it. They follow my orders and don't talk as much as your robot does."

"Yeah. We follow Grace's orders," Emma G. said.

"Yeah. We follow Grace's orders," Emma J. said.

"Yeah. And we don't talk too much," Emma G. said.

"Yeah. And we don't talk too much," Emma J. said.

"Yeah. We're good helpers," Emma G. said.

"Yeah. Good helpers. And good friends," Emma J. said.

Emma G. said "Yeah. Good —"

"Stop talking and bring me the box!" Grace yelled.

"Yeah. We'll just bring you the box," Emma G. said.

"Yeah. We'll just bring you the box," Emma J. said.

"Yeah. And we won't talk," Emma G. said.

"Yeah. We won't —"

"Stop talking!" Grace yelled.

The Emmas stopped talking. They carried the box to the front of the classroom.

I wondered what was in the box. I hoped it didn't contain people's faces. Grace Chang was evil. I had heard that she ripped the faces off of people who made her angry. I didn't know if that was true, but I didn't want to make her angry and find out.

Grace reached into the box with her long, sharp fingernails. She said, "I have been collecting these for many years. This first one is blood red."

Yikes! It really was a bloody, ripped-off face! I covered my eyes. I couldn't look at it.

"This next one is slimy. It felt good last week on my long, sharp fingernails," Grace said.

I kept my eyes shut tight.

ZEKE THE FREAK MEEKS, YOU'RE RUDE! DON'T COVER YOUR EYES DURING MY REPORT.

I slowly moved my hands from my eyes.

Phew. Grace wasn't holding ripped off faces. In her hands were bottles of red, slimy nail polish.

"I've spent many years collecting nail polish," she said. "I now have 152 bottles. That includes 37 shades of pink, 41 shades of red, nine different kinds of black, and many shades of ivory, white, and clear. Today I am wearing Fire Ant Red polish." She waved her long, sharp fingernails in the air.

I shuddered. I did not like fire or ants or fire ants. I did not like Grace's long, sharp fingernails. I really did not like watching them in motion. But it was better than looking at bloody, slimy, ripped-off faces.

Rudy Morse gave his report next. "I worked hard making sculptures," he said. He held up sculptures of a ballerina and a rose.

"Those are pretty. Are they made of clay?"
Laurie Schneider asked.

"No. They're made of dog doo. It's all from
my dog, Hulk. He's huge."

"*Eww*," Laurie said.

I thought they looked cool. I bet my cousin
Sam would like hearing about them today.
I raised my hand and asked, "Can I see the
sculptures up close?"

Mr. McNutty sighed. "Yes. But not too close.
And make sure you don't touch them."

I went to the front of the room for a close-up
view of the sculptures. "They look good," I said.

"Thanks," Rudy said. "I enjoy sculpting.
And my mom was happy I found her ruby ring
the day after Hulk ate it. It was in the middle of
a big pile of his dog doo."

"Thank you, Rudy. That's enough. Everyone seems to have worked hard on their projects," Mr. McNutty said.

Not everyone. I had not worked hard on my project. I had not worked on it at all. I did not even know what my project would be.

I groaned again.

Four Too Many RELATIVES

After school, I saw a bright red car parked in front of my house. The license plate was from Michigan. Hooray! My cousin Sam was here!

I threw open the front door and shouted, "Hello, hello, hello, everyone!"

My Aunt Wanda looked up from her magazine and said, "Zeke, you're just as loud as ever."

I smiled at her.

She didn't smile back.

My cousin Sam walked over and shook my hand. He said, "Good to see you. I hope you're doing well."

"Sam has taken manners classes. Zeke could use manners classes too. He could use a lot of manners classes," Aunt Wanda said.

While Aunt Wanda looked at my mother, I stuck out my tongue. I thought my manners were just fine. And manners classes seemed almost as boring as math classes.

PL + EASE = PLEASE

Uncle Wesley also shook my hand. He said, "I expected you to be as tall as Sam. You boys are the same age, but Sam is much bigger than you."

"Everyone grows at different rates," Mom said. Then she hugged me and asked, "How was school?"

"It was okay. Victoria Crow built a huge, talking robot and brought it to class," I said.

"That sounds like something Sam would do." Uncle Wesley patted Sam's back.

Sam shrugged.

"My friend Rudy made awesome sculptures out of dog doo. I got to see them up close," I said.

Sam frowned. "That sounds disgusting."

Uncle Wesley patted Sam on the back again.

"The kids in Zeke's class are sharing the special projects they worked on," Mom said.

"What's your project, Zeke?" Aunt Wanda asked.

"It's a secret," I said. It was a secret even from me.

"Last year, Sam composed a song and played it on his violin. It was quite advanced, but he performed wonderfully in front of his class," Uncle Wesley said.

"I'll show you a video of Sam playing the violin for an hour and a half without a break," Aunt Wanda said.

That seemed even more boring than manners classes. I said, "I don't have time to watch. I have a lot of homework. I need to work on my secret project and read a chapter of *The Black Stallion*."

"Sam read that entire book in one day."
Uncle Wesley beamed at Sam.

"Sometimes I read books in one day," I said.
Actually, I read picture books in one day, not
long novels like *The Black Stallion*.

"What do you like to do besides read?" Sam
asked me.

"I love video games. Do you want to play
one with me?"

"Video games!" Aunt Wanda gasped, as if I'd just asked Sam to play with sharks or matches or sharks holding matches. She said, "Video games are a waste of time. Sam has much better things to do. Right, Sam?"

Sam shrugged. "I guess so."

Having Sam here was not as much fun as I had hoped. So far, it wasn't fun at all.

My sister Mia ran out of her bedroom with my cousin Jen. Mia said, "We've been really busy."

Good. I had been hoping Jen would keep Mia too busy to sing Princess Sing-Along songs.

"Sit down and watch our show," Mia said.

"*Please* watch our show," Jen said.

"Jen took manners classes too," Aunt Wanda said.

Everyone sat down.

"Jen will dance while I sing Princess Sing-Along songs," Mia said.

Oh, no. I stood and said, "I need to do my homework."

Mom shook her head. "Be nice to your cousin and watch her dance. She's our guest."

I sighed and sat down. Then I asked Mom, "Where's Alexa? She should have to watch this too. I mean, she should *get* to watch this too."

"A few minutes after your cousins arrived, Alexa left the house. She remembered something she suddenly had to do," Mom said.

"I just remembered something I suddenly have to do," I said.

Mom crossed her arms. "You have to watch Mia and Jen's show."

"And now we begin," Mia said loudly.

Jen kicked her legs and spun around. I wouldn't really call that dancing. I'd call it flopping around.

Mia sang, "If you have mucus in your mouth, la la la, be careful where you spit it out, la la la. You wouldn't want it to land, la la la, on somebody's foot or hand, la la la."

I wouldn't really call that singing. I'd call it screeching.

Jen flopped around again while Mia screeched another song: "When you are someone's special guest, la la la, try not to be a bratty pest, la la la."

Everyone clapped.

"I'm confused about what a bratty pest is. I know what a brat is," Mia said.

"You sure do," I muttered.

"But what's a pest?" Mia asked.

Jen shrugged. "I don't know what a pest is, but I'm hungry. I need food right away."

Uncle Wesley told my mom, "I hope you bought the thirty items of food we asked for."

Aunt Wanda said, "It's chilly in this house. Someone should turn up the heat."

"Are you going to take us to see the sights?" Sam asked my mom. He gave her a stack of papers. "I made a long list of things I want to see."

My aunt, uncle, and cousins were great examples of pests.

I stood and said, "I'm going to my room to do homework."

Mom muttered, "I wish I had an excuse to go to my room."

I hurried to my bedroom and closed the door. I was glad to get away from my relatives.

Ow! I tripped over something on my rug.

Oh, no. It was a sleeping bag. Sam must be staying in my room.

I groaned again.

Don't Cry Over SPILLED MILK.

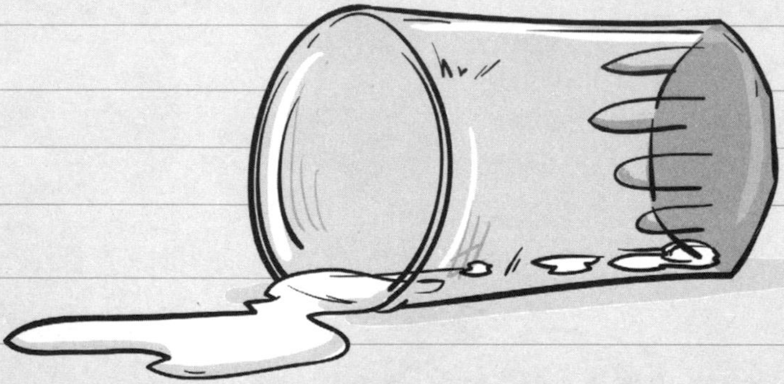

Even Better, DON'T SPILL THE MILK

I stayed in my room until dinnertime. Mom had cooked delicious meat loaf and French fries. She also served peas, brussels sprouts, and something Uncle Wesley had made. He called it Tofu-Bean Surprise. I wondered what the surprise was.

Mom told my sisters and me that we had to try all the food.

I did. I tried a huge hunk of meatloaf and a large handful of fries. They were totally delicious.

I also tried a small spoonful of the tofu-bean gunk, a brussels sprout, and a pea. They were totally gross.

Mom told me to put more healthy food on my plate. So I added another pea.

Sam filled his plate with the tofu-bean gunk, brussels sprouts, and peas.

"Maybe if Zeke ate healthier food, he'd grow as tall as Sam," Aunt Wanda said.

Sam ate a big forkful of the tofu-bean gunk. He said, "This Tofu-Bean Surprise is really tasty."

Now I knew what the surprise was. It was surprising that anyone liked the tofu-bean gunk.

I said, "Yes, this Tofu-Bean Surprise is really tasty. It's full of taste." Full of the taste of old boots, wood chips, and cardboard. I had never actually tried old boots or wood chips.

But I had tried cardboard. Last year, my friend Rudy had paid me a dollar to eat a big piece of his notebook. That old cardboard notebook had tasted better than the tofu-bean gunk.

I needed to wash away the horrible taste in my mouth. I reached for my cup of milk.

It fell over. Milk spilled on the table and onto Aunt Wanda's lap.

"Sorry," I said. I looked around the table for a napkin.

Before I could find one, Sam gave Aunt Wanda a roll of paper towels and stain remover.

"Thank you for your help, Sam," Aunt Wanda said. She smiled at him. Then she glared at me.

"Accidents happen," Mom said.

"I will find Zeke a good manners class," Aunt Wanda said.

"No!" I shouted. Then I took a deep breath. "I mean, no, thank you."

"No, thank you," Mom repeated.

I crawled under the table to clean the spilled milk. I stayed there, taking a break from my relatives.

My dog lay under the table too, eating a big mound of tofu-bean gunk. I wondered who had put it there.

"A manners class would teach Zeke that it's rude to sit under the table during dinnertime," Aunt Wanda said.

I returned to my chair. Sam's plate was empty. Maybe he was a very fast eater. Or maybe he had given his tofu-bean gunk to Waggles.

When we were all done eating, Sam said, "I'll wash everyone's dishes."

Uncle Wesley patted his back. "You're so helpful."

I went into the kitchen and said, "I can help you wash the dishes."

"No, thank you," Sam said.

His voice sounded muffled because his mouth was full of food. Hmm. That food looked like French fries and cookies. I bet he was hungry after giving his healthy dinner to Waggles. I also bet he'd lied when he said the tofu-bean gunk was tasty.

I returned to my bedroom, away from my phony cousin.

A while later, Mom knocked on my door. She said, "Your friends are here. They're waiting in the living room for you."

Oops. I forgot I'd invited my best friend, Hector Cruz, and my second best friend, Charlie Marple, to meet Sam. I had told them Sam was cool. That was before I knew how uncool he really was.

I ran out of my room. I hoped Sam wasn't making my friends too miserable.

Hector and Charlie were sitting on the couch next to Sam. They were laughing. It wasn't nice to laugh at him, no matter how awful he was.

"Hi. I see you met my cousin Sam," I said.

"He knows a lot of jokes," Hector said.

Charlie nodded. "He's really funny."

"Sam has a great sense of humor," Uncle Wesley said.

Sam kept telling jokes. Hector and Charlie kept laughing.

I sat by myself. No one paid attention to me.

Waggles came into the room. He wore a pink sweater. He looked very silly. I whistled for him anyway, and he ran over. Then he kept running, stopped in front of Sam, and curled up next to him.

Even my dog thought Sam was better than me.

Sam told another joke.

Waggles licked him.

Hector and Charlie laughed again.

I kicked the coffee table.

Ow! I hurt my toe.

Just Another Day at School, EXCEPT FOR THE

WILD UPROAR

Sam's parents thought he was perfect. But I found out he had a fault: he snored. But he didn't just snore. He snored really loudly, with heavy breaths, shrill whistles, and noisy snorts. It sounded like trains, farm animals, and a marching band were running through my bedroom all night. I hardly got any sleep.

So I was really tired when my alarm clock went off. But for once in my life, I couldn't wait to go to school. I wanted to get away from my relatives.

I walked into my classroom before school started. I was so early that only two other kids were in the room: Laurie Schneider and Victoria Crow.

Laurie waved to me and said, "Zeke, come here."

I went to her desk. A large box sat on top of it.

"This is my big homework project. Ta-da!" Laurie pulled off the lid of the box. Inside the box, three brown, fuzzy caterpillars slithered on green leaves.

Yikes! Bugs! I am afraid of all kinds of bugs — even ants, ladybugs, and caterpillars. I never told anyone that. I didn't want to get teased.

"Would you like to hold Rainbow, Sunshine, and Starlight?" Laurie asked.

I was too scared to talk.

"Rainbow, Sunshine, and Starlight are the names of my caterpillars. They're so soft and fuzzy. Pet them," Laurie said.

I was still too scared to talk. I shook my head.

Victoria walked over with her robot. She said, "That caterpillar project is good. But it's not as good as my robot. No one can do a better project than me, because I'm the smartest kid in third grade."

"Why did you bring your annoying robot today? You already did your report," I said.

"I am not annoying. *Beep.*" The annoying robot pointed at me and said, "You are rude. Also, you are annoying."

"I brought Robot Rupert to school today to remind everyone how smart I am. I am the only kid in third grade smart enough to build a robot." Victoria pointed to the robot and said, "Do some more cleaning."

Robot Rupert said, "You did not say please. That was rude. *Beep.*"

Then Rupert stretched his metal arms wide, opened his claw, and zoomed around the classroom. He grabbed pencils and papers from kids' desks and flung them across the room.

"Knock it off," Victoria said.

"I will. I will knock lots of things off," Rupert replied. He knocked over the comic book that Hector had hidden inside his math book. Then he hurled lunch boxes onto the floor, leaving a mess of fruit salad, chips, and the pea soup that Nicole Finkle's mom always made for her and Nicole never ate.

"Stop," Victoria said.

Rupert kept going. He reached his claw high up on the classroom wall, pulled off Mr. McNutty's "Dare to Aim High" poster, and shredded it.

"Stop!" Victoria screamed.

Mr. McNutty ran into the room along with most of my classmates.

"Whoa!" Aaron Glass exclaimed.

"Cool," Rudy Morse said.

"Shut that thing off," Mr. McNutty said.

Grace pointed at Victoria with her long, sharp fingernail. "Keep your robot away from my nail polish collection," she warned.

"None of you said *please*. You are rude. *Beep*," Robot Rupert said.

Maybe manners classes were useful after all.

Rupert rushed to Grace's giant box of nail polish.

Grace said, "Leave that alone."

"You still did not say please. That is rude. *Beep*," Rupert said.

"Please!" Grace screamed.

"You screamed. That is also rude," Rupert said. He pulled the bottles from the box and threw them all over the room. The bottles smashed and polish flew everywhere.

"I'll rip that robot's face off," Grace said.

"No you will not. *Beep.* My face is made of metal. It cannot be ripped off," Rupert said.

"Turn off that robot, Victoria," Mr. McNutty said.

Victoria pressed the button on Rupert's belly and switched him off.

The classroom was a mess. Pea soup, broken bottles, papers, books, crayons, pencils, food, and "Dare to Aim High" poster scraps lay all over the place. Red nail polish dotted my shirt. White polish covered Victoria's face. Pink polish streaked Mr. McNutty's hairpiece.

I whispered to Hector, "I'm glad the robot got out of control. Now we won't have time for math lessons."

Laurie Schneider said, "Oh, no! I opened the lid of my caterpillar box just before Robot Rupert went wild. In all the excitement, I forgot to put the lid back on. One of my caterpillars escaped."

I was no longer glad the robot got out of control. There was nothing scarier than a caterpillar loose in the classroom.

"Oh. I was wrong about one of my caterpillars escaping," Laurie said.

Phew. No more worries.

"It wasn't just *one* of my caterpillars. *Two* of them escaped. Rainbow and Starlight are both on the loose."

Yikes!

"Oh. I was wrong again. Rainbow and Starlight didn't escape," Laurie said.

Phew. No more worries.

"Rainbow and *Sunshine* escaped."

Yikes!

"Never mind. I see them," Laurie said.

Phew.

"They're crawling up Zeke's back," she said.

Yikes!

"Stay where you are. I'll pluck the caterpillars off you," Laurie said.

I stayed where I was and tried not to shake too much.

Laurie slowly walked over. She said, "Does anyone have a camera? The caterpillars crawling up Zeke's shirt have made a little heart. It's so cute! This would make a great picture."

"Just get them off me," I said, trying not to sound scared. Then I added, "Please."

"Ooh, one of them is about to crawl up your neck," Laurie said.

"Please, please, please hurry and get them off me," I politely begged.

Finally, Laurie put her hand on my back and said, "Okay, I got them. My caterpillars must really like you, Zeke. Do you want to pet them?"

"No. No, thank you," I said. I couldn't wait for school to end.

Actually, yes, I could wait. Because after school, Sam and his family would still be at my house.

No One CARES About Adults

The only thing that I care about right now is this sandwich.

A few hours later, I ate lunch with my friends Hector and Charlie.

Hector said, "Zeke, you seemed scared of Laurie's caterpillars."

I was embarrassed about being scared of bugs. I was super embarrassed about being scared of caterpillars. They were soft and furry, moved slowly, and didn't even bite or sting or fly. But they still terrified me. I said, "Who me? Scared?"

Hector nodded. "Yes, you."

"Were you scared of the caterpillars?" Charlie asked.

"Who, me?" I asked.

Charlie nodded. "Yes, you."

I bit into my sandwich. Then I changed the subject. I asked, "Do you think I need a manners class?"

"You're talking with your mouth full," Hector said.

"And you have jelly dripping down your chin," Charlie said.

"Don't change the subject. Tell me if I need a manners class," I said.

Hector burped. "Who cares about manners?"

Charlie licked applesauce from her fingers. "Adults care about manners. But who cares about adults?"

"My cousin Sam has good manners," I said. "He also eats healthy food, washes people's dishes, plays the violin, writes music, and makes people laugh."

"Really?" Hector asked as he pulled some wax from his ear.

Charlie picked at a scab. "Your cousin does all that?"

I nodded. "He made you guys laugh a lot yesterday."

"He didn't make us laugh. We were laughing to be polite," Charlie said.

"Yeah. If someone tells jokes, it's polite to laugh. You don't need a manners class to know that," Hector said.

"I thought that you thought Sam was really funny," I said.

"I thought that you thought Sam should think we thought he was really funny," Charlie said.

"Huh?" I asked.

Charlie shrugged. "You seemed happy about having your cousin visit. And I wanted to be polite. So I laughed at his dumb jokes."

"Me too," Hector said.

I sighed. "I'm not very happy about my cousin now. He isn't as great as I thought he'd be. And he isn't as great as his parents think he is. Sam isn't perfect. Don't tell anyone, but he snores really loudly."

"Nobody's perfect," Charlie said.

"If Sam didn't try to act like he was perfect, I'd like him more," I said.

"I like you guys, even though you're not perfect," Hector said.

"Same here," I said. Then I realized something. I bet if my friends ever found out my biggest secret, that I was terrified of bugs, they'd still like me.

I decided to tell them. I said, "I have something to tell you. Something about myself. Something I've been keeping a secret. Something that may surprise you. Something unusual. Something —"

The bell rang.

I still had three more "something"s left before telling my big secret. But we had to get back to class.

When I got home from school, Aunt Wanda looked at me and frowned. "Zeke, did you brush your hair today? It looks like a dirty old mop fell on your head and decided to stay there."

Insulting people was bad manners. Aunt Wanda needed manners classes. But I didn't say that to her, because that would have insulted her and been bad manners.

Mom said, "Zeke brushes his hair every day. He runs around with his friends on the school playground. So sometimes his hair gets a bit messy."

Aunt Wanda raised her eyebrows. "A *bit* messy?"

Mom glared at her. "Yes. A bit."

Jen and Mia ran into the living room. Mia said, "Oh, good. Zeke's home. Now that everyone's here, it's show time again."

"Darn it," my sister Alexa said in a fake sad voice. "I need to leave right away. Sorry I'll have to miss your show."

Mia said, "Don't worry, Alexa. We'll repeat our show for you when you get back. You can watch it for the first time and everyone else can watch it twice."

I groaned.

Today's show was even worse than yesterday's. Jen danced by flinging her arms and legs all over the place. Her flailing arms just missed hitting our TV. She kicked our glass candy dish off the coffee table. Luckily, I caught it before it crashed to the ground.

Meanwhile, Mia screeched a Princess Sing-Along song: "If you do not brush your hair, la la la, weird things could start living there, la la la. Your tangled mess of hair could house, la la la, a bug or bird turd or a mouse, la la la."

Both of the girls bowed, and everyone clapped.

I needed to get away. "Do you want to play basketball with me, Sam?" I asked.

He frowned. "I'm not good at basketball."

"That doesn't matter. We'll play just for fun," I said.

"Fun?" he asked, as if he'd never heard that word before.

Uncle Wesley shook his head. "It's too cold to go outside."

"We'll wear jackets. Come on, Sam," I said.

"Is it safe out there?" Aunt Wanda asked.

"Yes. They'll be right in front of the house," Mom said.

I ran outside and got my basketball.

Sam followed me.

I made a basket. Then I threw the ball to Sam.

He missed it. He ran after it, grabbed it, brought it near the basket, and took a shot. He missed the basket. Sam had been right. He wasn't good at basketball.

"If I tried harder, I could make all the shots I want," he said.

"I don't care whether you get the ball in the basket or not. I just want to have fun hanging out and running around," I said. "Anyway, I know you're good at other stuff. Your mom said you wrote songs and played the violin really well. And you read *The Black Stallion* in one day and knew lots of jokes to tell my friends. Plus, you have great manners and eat healthy food."

Sam nodded. "That's true. And if I practice every day, I can get good at basketball."

I tossed the ball to Sam. "Or don't practice and just play for fun."

"Things aren't fun unless you're good at them."

I shrugged. "They're fun for me."

"You're just saying that because you're not good at anything."

That made me angry. I stole the ball from Sam and made a perfect shot.

"Lucky shot," Sam said.

"Good shot. I'm good at lots of things: basketball, video games, and putting up with mean cousins," I said.

"Me? I'm not mean," Sam said.

I dribbled the ball. "You lie to people so you can act like you're better than them."

"I *am* better than *you*. And I never lie."

I shook my head.

"The only thing you're better at is being a big phony. I don't believe you read *The Black Stallion* in one day. I bet you saw the movie instead. And I know the real reason you went into the kitchen to wash dishes. I caught you with your mouth full of French fries and cookies. You lied when you said the tofu-bean gunk was tasty. At dinner last night, I saw my dog under the table, eating your Tofu-Bean Surprise. That's why he snuggled up to you on the couch later . . . to get more food. Also, those jokes you told my friends weren't funny."

Sam's eyes narrowed. "At least I do my homework and use good manners and make my parents proud."

"My mom is proud of me too. And I don't have to pretend to be great at everything."

"I'm sick of you. Goodbye!" Sam yelled. He hurried inside the house.

"I'm sicker of you! I'll stay here and have a ton of fun without you!" I yelled.

But being outside by myself wasn't a ton of fun. It wasn't even a pound of fun. It was barely an ounce of fun.

THE IMPORTANT THINGS IN LIFE:

Fake Coughs, WEIRD FACES, and Underarm FARTS

MATH

Math homework is NOT one of the important things in life.

Unless you can trick your cousin into doing it for you!

Once I returned to the house, Aunt Wanda said, "I hope Sam taught you some basketball skills. He's a great athlete."

Uncle Wesley patted Sam on the back.

Sam frowned and stared at the floor.

"Eating healthy food like the Tofu-Bean Surprise makes him strong," Aunt Wanda said.

Sam kept frowning and staring at the floor.

Mia grabbed my arm. She said, "It's time for our new Princess Sing-Along song and dance show."

Ugh. Not again. I had to stop this. I told Mia, "You should practice very hard. After a few hours of practice, your next show will be perfect."

"Okay. Here we go," Mia said.

Jen jumped up and down and flailed around.

Mia sang in a screechy voice, "Everybody will agree, la la la. It's fun to visit family, la la la."

"Not everybody will agree," Sam said, crossing his arms.

"I won't agree." I crossed my arms too.

"I'll keep singing the song over and over until you agree," Mia said.

"And I'll keep dancing and dancing and dancing," Jen said.

"When I told you to practice, I meant to do it in your bedroom, with the door closed," I said. "That way, we'll be surprised when you perform your perfect show later."

"Oh. Okay," Mia said. She and Jen went to Mia's room and closed the door behind them.

Finally. Now maybe I would get a little time to myself.

"Zeke, now you can watch the video of Sam playing the violin for an hour and a half," Aunt Wanda said.

"I don't have time to watch a video now," I said.

"You should watch it soon. You won't believe how talented Sam is," Uncle Wesley said.

I rolled my eyes. "You're right. I won't believe it."

Once again, Sam frowned and stared at the floor.

"Did I tell you he writes songs too? And sometimes he reads entire books in one day," Aunt Wanda said.

"You told me both those things, and many other great things about Sam," I said.

"We're proud of him," Aunt Wanda said.

"He's great." Uncle Wesley patted Sam's back again. Sam kept frowning and staring at the floor.

I went to my room and sat on my bed.

Sam followed me and sat on my desk chair. He said, "I'm sorry. You were right. I didn't really read *The Black Stallion* in one day. I saw the movie in one day. And I fed Waggles my Tofu-Bean Surprise. It tasted nasty. You were also right about why I washed the dishes. I wanted to sneak junk food from the kitchen. I'm not as good as my parents think I am."

I couldn't be mad at Sam anymore. I felt kind of bad for him. I told him, "You're great. You're a good cousin. And you're smart. I wish I had thought of giving Waggles the tofu-bean gunk. You also have a lot of talents that I don't have, like playing the violin and writing songs."

"It was only one song, and my parents wrote most of it." Sam sighed. "You're really good at basketball."

"Thanks. I'm good at other things too," I said. "I'm great at getting out of chores. Sometimes I do a chore really badly on purpose. Then my mom decides it's easier to do it herself. Sometimes I tell my classmates that a chore is fun. Then they want to do the chore for me. Or I pretend I'm too sick to do chores." I showed Sam my fake cough and phony weak voice.

"Wow, you really do sound sick," Sam said. He tried a fake cough. It wasn't very good. But he got better at it with my help.

"I'm also good at making weird faces to scare my little sister," I said.

"I'm good at that too," Sam said. He made his eyes buggy, as if they were jumping out of his head. It looked so weird that it even scared me a little.

He showed me how to do it. I couldn't wait to scare Mia with it.

Then I taught Sam how to make fart noises with his underarms.

"You're very talented," Sam said.

"I'm bad at math. Are you good at it?" I asked.

Sam nodded. "I'm pretty good at math."

"Prove it." I put my math book in front of Sam and gave him a pencil and paper. "Let's see how fast you can do the problems on this page. It will be fun. I'll time you."

Sam did the math problems while I played with my yo-yo. After he finished, he asked, "How was that?"

I grinned. "We both did well. You did the math problems in 22 minutes. And I got you to do my homework. Thanks."

"You really *are* good at getting out of chores," Sam said.

"Now that my math homework is done, I have time for a video game," I said. "Do you want to play *Hit Everything that Moves*?"

Sam frowned. "I don't know how to play video games. I probably won't be good at it."

"That doesn't matter. I'll teach you," I said.

We went into the living room. I turned on my game player and gave Sam a controller.

"Video games are a waste of time," Aunt Wanda said.

"Having fun isn't a waste of time," Sam said.

We played for a while. Sam was a fast learner and we had fun.

Our parents made us stop for dinner. Uncle Wesley had cooked Green Grain Delight. He should have called it Green Grain Fright. It was even grosser than the Tofu-Bean Surprise. Sam and I fed it to Waggles under the table.

After dinner, we went to the kitchen and took turns doing dishes. During my turn, Sam ate a bunch of potato chips. During his turn, I ate chocolate-covered pretzels.

Once we were done, Mia said, "Jen and I practiced singing and dancing." She stopped and took a deep breath. "We practiced for hours and hours to make it perfect, just like Zeke told us." She sat on a chair and took another deep breath. "We're ready to start our show."

Alexa said, "I need to do something very important. Sorry I have to miss your show again." Then she rushed out the front door.

Everyone else sat down to watch Mia and Jen's show. I hoped my plan would work.

Mia said, "We . . ." She took a few deep breaths. "We will do our . . ." She took another deep breath. "Here's our show." She started singing very quietly.

Jen jumped in the air. Then she fell on the rug. She stayed there.

"Are you all right?" Aunt Wanda asked her.

Jen shook her head. She looked terrible.

"We practiced and practiced for such a long time. Now I'm too tired to dance."

Mia sat on the rug next to Jen. "After all that practicing, my voice is too tired to sing. We can't do a show tonight."

Sam whispered, "Good job, Zeke. Your plan worked."

I felt so proud, I patted myself on the back.

"We'll do an extra long show tomorrow," Mia said.

I groaned.

"Did you just rudely groan?" Aunt Wanda asked.

"That wasn't Zeke groaning. It was the dog," Sam said.

"Oh, all right," she said.

I tried not to laugh.

Sam put his hands over his mouth, but a giggle escaped.

"Did you hear that?" I said. "The dog is giggling now. Waggles sure is rude. He needs manners classes."

Aunt Wanda glared at me.

Sam and I burst out laughing. Then we made weird faces at each other and laughed some more.

That night, Sam and I played video games again. After Sam destroyed a giant red alligator, I said, "You've improved a lot."

"You're a good teacher. I want to buy video games to play at home," Sam said.

"You can play with them here on vacation. But not at home. They're a waste of time," Aunt Wanda said.

"Have you done all your homework, Zeke?" Mom asked.

"My math homework is done," I said. I didn't tell her that Sam had done it for me.

"What about your big project?"

I sighed. It was due tomorrow. I still hadn't started it.

Mom turned off the game console. "When is your project due, Zeke?"

"Not for a long time," I said. There were 60 seconds in a minute, and 60 minutes in an hour. Since school didn't start for another 12 hours or so, my project was due thousands of seconds from now. That seemed like a long time.

"Do you still want to show the class your video game skills?" Mom asked me.

I frowned.

"You said I couldn't do that," I said.

"I changed my mind. I realized you worked hard to get better at something you love. And you showed your cousin how to play. I'm proud of you for that. You should be proud too. I'm sorry I didn't realize that sooner," Mom said.

"That's okay. No one's perfect," I told her.

"That's true. No one's perfect," Sam said. "Zeke is good at a lot of things, but he snores really loudly."

Sam nodded. "At least you admit it."

"Sam, will you go to school with me tomorrow? I want to show my class what I taught you," I said.

"Sam has plans tomorrow. We're going to the shoe museum." Uncle Wesley said.

Aunt Wanda smiled. "We'll learn all about the history of shoes: loafers, sneakers, sandals, boots. After that, we'll go to the soap museum or the pencil museum to learn about soap or pencils."

"I'd rather go to Zeke's school," Sam said.

"We can look at all my classmates' shoes. And we can see soap in the school bathroom and pencils in my classroom," I said.

"Please let me go with Zeke tomorrow," Sam said.

Finally, Aunt Wanda shrugged. "All right. You might learn something at Zeke's school. And you'll be away from that awful video game."

"Video games aren't awful. I'll show you and Uncle Wesley how to play," I said.

My aunt shook her head. "I won't like them."

My uncle shook his head too. "I'm too old for video games."

"Give them a try," my mom said.

They did.

They liked playing video games.

They liked playing video games a lot.

In fact, they liked video games too much. They laughed and squealed and shouted. It was annoying.

They were so loud that they woke Mia. She came out of her bedroom and said, "I'm in the middle of a crazy dream. In my dream, Aunt Wanda and Uncle Wesley are acting different, like they're having fun. Hey, my voice feels better. Let me try singing a Princess Sing-Along song."

Before I could stop her, Mia rubbed her eyes and screeched, "You may wake to a surprise, la la la. Yucky stuff around your eyes, la la la. Call it eye boogers or crust, la la la, mucus, discharge, or eye dust, la la la."

"Go back to bed, Mia," Mom said.

"I just attacked a flying octopus!" Uncle Wesley waved around the video game controller.

"Watch out for that angry purple rabbit!" Aunt Wanda warned.

Mia rubbed her eyes again and said, "This is the strangest dream ever." Then she went back to bed.

"Spending too much time playing video games is bad for you, Uncle Wesley and Aunt Wanda. You should stop," I said.

"Zeke is right. You should stop playing and give us a turn," Sam said.

Aunt Wanda and Uncle Wesley ignored us and kept playing their game. Actually, it was my game. But they ignored me when I told them that. They were being rude. They needed manners classes.

"I bet your parents will be hogging my video game all night," I told Sam.

He groaned.

BEST
HOMEWORK
Project
EVER

HIT EVERYTHING THAT MOVES

If all my schoolwork was this fun, I might actually like doing my homework.

The next day, I brought four great things to school:

- My video game console.

- My game controllers.

- My *Hit Everything that Moves* game.

- My cousin Sam.

I gave my report first thing in the morning. I told the class, "I played *Hit Everything that Moves* for many weeks. It's a very hard game. But after a lot of practice, I got good at it. Watch this."

I played the game for a few minutes. I traveled to three strange worlds and destroyed five horrible creatures.

Next, I brought Sam up and said, "This is my cousin Sam. His parents think he is smart and has great manners and eats healthy food all the time. He's smart, but I don't know about those other things. Also, he snores really loudly. I don't care. I like Sam because he's nice and fun to be around."

"I like Zeke too, even though he snores much louder than me, and even though he tricked me into doing his math homework," Sam said.

Mr. McNutty frowned.

"Zeke tricked me into doing his math homework a few weeks ago," Rudy Morse said.

"He tricked me into doing his spelling homework," Laurie Schneider said.

I quickly changed the subject. "Let's get back to my report. Sam is nine years old. Until yesterday, he had never played a video game."

"Never?" Hector gasped.

"Not even once?" Rudy asked.

"I don't mean to be rude, but is Sam from another planet?" Aaron Glass asked.

Mr. McNutty told everyone to be quiet.

I continued with my report. "Yesterday, I showed Sam how to play *Hit Everything that Moves.*"

"Zeke is a great teacher," Sam said.

"Thanks. I taught Sam how to hold the controller and what buttons to press."

"He didn't even know how to hold the controller?" Hector gasped again.

"Not at all?" Rudy asked.

"Hector and Rudy, do you want to stay inside for lunch?" Mr. NcNutty said.

Hector smiled. "I would love to. As long as we can play Zeke's video game."

"Me too," Rudy said. "Playing video games would be a great lunch break."

"No, you can't play games during lunchtime. Be quiet and listen to Zeke's report," Mr. McNutty said.

"I helped Sam get good at the game. Watch us play," I said.

Sam and I played *Hit Everything that Moves*.

We got so involved in the game that we forgot all about the report.

"Zeke, are you [...] th your report?"
Mr. McNutty asked.

That distracted us. I got swallowed by a
two-headed rattlesnake. Sam got stung by a
poisonous piglet. "We both just died in the
game. But nobody's perfect," I said.

Everyone clapped for us. Some of my
classmates said it was the best report ever. A lot
of kids said they wished they had thought of
doing that.

Mr. McNutty said, "That video game project was, uh, well . . . interesting. From now on, everyone will need my approval before starting new projects. I don't want this type of thing to happen again. Though it was, uh, well . . . interesting."

He turned to Sam and said, "You are welcome to stay with our class today. After Aaron and Nicole give their reports, we will practice spelling. Then we'll work on fractions and writing in cursive. After that, we'll read a chapter from the science textbook."

Sam said, "That sounds, uh, well . . . interesting. I would love to stay here today."

He *would*? That stuff didn't sound interesting to me. It all seemed extremely boring.

"But there's a problem. I'm not feeling well," Sam said in a weak voice.

Sam's weak voice sounded fake, just the way we'd practiced yesterday.

Then he faked a cough, exactly like I had taught him.

"You seem sick. Get your parents to pick you up, Sam," Mr. McNutty said.

I thought about pretending to be sick too. But I wanted to see the last two reports. So far, watching the reports had been fun.

Aunt Wanda and Uncle Wesley came to our classroom quickly. Aunt Wanda said, "We'll bring the video game and console back to Zeke's house. We were going to tour the fabric museum. But since Sam isn't feeling well, we'll stay home and play the video game. I mean, we'll stay home and take care of Sam."

"Sam is too sick to play video games. He'll have to rest while we play," Uncle Wesley said.

Sam frowned.

I whispered to him, "When you get to my house, go to my bedroom. There's a handheld video game device in the top drawer of my dresser. Have fun with it."

Sam thanked me and left the classroom.

Mr. McNutty said, "Now for the last two reports, from Aaron and Nicole."

"I brought in my ant farm." Aaron held up a glass case filled with scary red and black ants.

"I brought in my spiders." Nicole held up a plastic tub containing three huge, hairy, red-eyed spiders.

I coughed and said in a weak voice, "I feel sick."

Mr. McNutty shook his head. "Zeke, I've heard your phony cough and phony weak voice a lot this year. Don't pretend you're sick like your cousin did."

"You knew Sam was pretending?" I asked.

Mr. McNutty nodded. "Of course. Now let's get started on the reports. Everyone will get a close-up view of the ants and spiders."

I groaned again.

ABOUT THE AUTHOR

D. L. Green lives in California with her husband, three children, silly dog, and a big collection of rubber chickens. She loves to read, write, and joke around.

ABOUT THE ILLUSTRATOR

Josh Alves got to spend his summers swimming and having water balloon fights with his cousins. Josh gets to draw in his studio in Maine where he lives with his wonderful wife and their four lovely children.

DO YOU THINK I NEED TO TAKE MANNERS CLASSES?

(And other really important questions)

Write answers to these questions, or discuss them with your friends and classmates.

1. Do you think I need to take manners classes like Sam? What could they possibly teach me?!

2. Have you ever met someone who pretended to be perfect? What makes them NOT perfect?

3. Being scared of caterpillars is super embarrassing. Are you scared of anything? Are you embarrassed about your fear?

4. Some people, like my Aunt Wanda, think that video games are a waste of time. What do you think?

5. Sometimes it can be really fun to have relatives visit. Sometimes it's really annoying. What is it like when your relatives visit you?

BIG WORDS
according to Zeke

TRY USING THEM IN SENTENCES JUST LIKE I DO

ANNOYING: Things that are annoying bug you so much you think you might lose it!

DESPISE: If you hate something more than anything you have ever, ever, ever hated before, then you actually despise it.

DISCHARGE: Something gross that oozes out of your body, like eye gunk or pus.

DISGUSTING: Things that make you go "EW!" like love notes, most girls, and liver.

DISTRACTED: In awe of something (like a video game) so much so that you don't notice anything else going on around you.

EMBARRASSED: The feeling you have after people notice something about you that you don't want them to know, like being afraid of bugs.

GASP: A noise a person makes when they are shocked — like Aunt Wanda when I asked Sam to play video games with me.

HURL: If you hurl something, it's probably because you're angry, like when the robot hurled things on the floor because Victoria was rude to him.

Tofu-bean gunk is disgusting.
But Waggles seems to LOVE it.

IDIOT: Someone who is really dumb.

IGNORED: When I get ignored, people act like they can't hear me or even see me. RUDE!

INSULT: To say or do something that makes a person feel bad. Note: I said a PERSON, not Princess Sing-Along!

INVISIBLE: Impossible to see, like the invisible rocket ship I'm building for my next class project.

MISSION: A very important job to do.

MUCUS: Slimy, wet stuff that comes out of your nose and eyes. This stuff includes boogers and eye boogers.

PUNISHMENT: This happens when I do something wrong or behave badly. Parents and teachers like to give out punishments like missing recess or being grounded for the weekend, even for silly things like making an invisible rocket ship.

SNUGGLE: To lie close to someone. Waggles does this. So does Mia sometimes. It can be very annoying.

SQUEAL: This high-pitched sound usually comes from little girls and puppies and often annoys everyone who hears it. This week, I heard it come from two grown adults — my Aunt Wanda and Uncle Wesley.

The Great Puke Fake-Out

Want to be the ultimate master of faking sick? You'll need some props to help you out. And fake vomit is just the ticket to a day off of school, lounging on the couch and playing video games. Or you can use your fake vomit to prank your brother or sister.

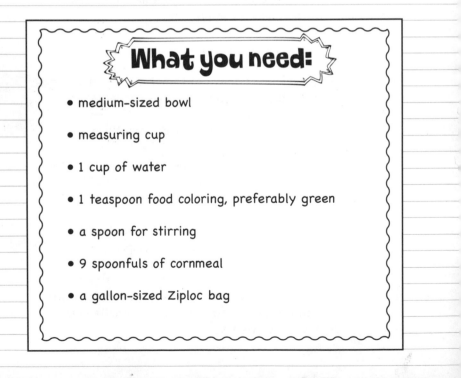

What you need:

- medium-sized bowl

- measuring cup

- 1 cup of water

- 1 teaspoon food coloring, preferably green

- a spoon for stirring

- 9 spoonfuls of cornmeal

- a gallon-sized Ziploc bag

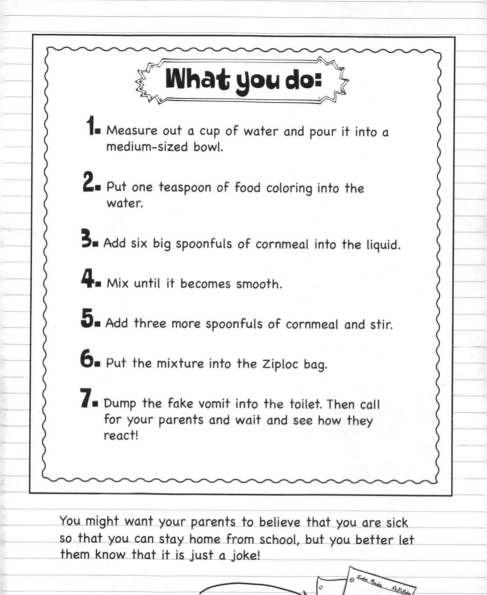

What you do:

1. Measure out a cup of water and pour it into a medium-sized bowl.

2. Put one teaspoon of food coloring into the water.

3. Add six big spoonfuls of cornmeal into the liquid.

4. Mix until it becomes smooth.

5. Add three more spoonfuls of cornmeal and stir.

6. Put the mixture into the Ziploc bag.

7. Dump the fake vomit into the toilet. Then call for your parents and wait and see how they react!

You might want your parents to believe that you are sick so that you can stay home from school, but you better let them know that it is just a joke!

My next report topic: VOMIT, The History of Puke

MY REPORT